This book is dedicated to my beautiful family. Laura, Taylor, Brianna, Landon, Mike, Monique, Brittney, and all my beautiful grandkids.

Order this book online at www.trafford.com
or email orders@trafford.com

Most Trafford titles are also available at major online book retailers.

© Copyright 2012 Jack E. Nelson.

All rights reserved. No part of this publication may be reproduced, stored in a retrieval system, or transmitted, in any form or by any means, electronic, mechanical, photocopying, recording, or otherwise, without the written prior permission of the author.

Illustrations by Dwight Nacaytuna

Printed in the United States of America.

ISBN: 978-1-4669-5466-3(sc)

978-1-4669-5465-6(e)

Library of Congress Control Number: 2012920451

Trafford rev. 11/01/2012

www.trafford.com

North America & international
toll-free: 1 888 232 4444 (USA & Canada)
phone: 250 383 6864   fax: 812 355 4082

Space Rocks

Jack E. Nelson

Illustrations by
Dwight Nacaytuna

Shooting Star, Asteroid, and Comet had just spent the morning watching the sun come up. "It is so cool watching the sunrise!" said Star. "I agree," said Asteroid. Comet said, "I like to wear special glasses that keep the sun's ultraviolet rays from burning my eyes. I love to feel the heat. It is nice and warm." Let's start from the beginning, on how our three friends came to be.

Shooting Star, just a baby at one million years old, was born in the Milky Way. There, she had a very close family with many brothers and sisters. They always had tons of fun together. Everything was going terrific, until one day the galaxy exploded and Shooting Star was shot out into the UNIVERSE away from her family.

Asteroid was born about five million years ago. He also had lots of brothers and sisters, and they all would cruise the UNIVERSE together checking out all the planets and solar system. One day, they ran into a planet named Jupiter, and it caused them to be separated from each other. Asteroid was pushed one way and his family was pulled another way.

Comet was about ten million years old. He didn't have any brothers or sisters but had spent most of his life traveling through the solar system, dodging stars, planets, suns, and black holes. He knew he had to be very careful around the black holes because if he got too close, it could suck him right up. Every fifty years or so, Comet would ride by Earth.

Star, Comet, and Asteroid all met each other one day while cruising through the solar system. They were all amazed and happy to have found each other after being separated from their families and had hope in finding more space rocks. So from then on, they decided to stick together and travel the UNIVERSE as a new family.

The next morning, they decided to go exploring. The three friends made a pack that they would stick together forever and explore the UNIVERSE. They set out on their first adventure together to the red planet, Mars, the fourth planet from the sun. They headed out early on their mission, and on the way there, they dodged meteorites and space junk. One of the meteorites barely missed Comet and Star. They figured it was going to be a scary mission.

Finally, after traveling many hours, they landed safely on Mars and were very excited. They couldn't wait to go exploring the big red planet. As they started exploring, they found a big giant canyon. "Wow!" they exclaimed. "What could we do here?" Asteroid asked hopefully. This would be an awesome place to play some baseball, they all thought. Asteroid decided to bat while Star pitched and Comet played outfield. On the first pitch, Star threw a curveball. Asteroid swung and missed. "Strike!" said Comet. Then Star threw a fastball, and Asteroid swung and missed again. "Strike 2!" said Comet. The next pitch, Star threw another fastball; and Asteroid hit it, long and far. "Wow!" said Star. The ball traveled so fast it had sparks coming off it. Comet ran after the ball and leaped in the air and caught it. "You're out!" Star shouted.

They played for another hour or so. The next time Asteroid hit the ball, it went all the way to outer space. "That was so fun," said the three new friends. "Let's take a break and drink some water."

After they rested, Comet suggested they go climb the canyon wall. The canyon walls were huge and very steep. Comet tied a rope around himself to help Star and Asteroid up the steep parts. Comet climbed up halfway then dropped the rope back for Star and Asteroid. "That looks scary," said Star. "Don't worry, I'll pull you up," said Comet. Asteroid and Comet grabbed a hold of the rope, and Comet lifted them up the steep canyon wall. Comet then used the rope to lasso the huge rock at the top of the canyon, and then they all pulled themselves up. "Yeah, we made it!" they all shouted happily.

After a short rest, Star looked up at the Olympus Mons, the largest volcanic mountain in the solar system. "Let's go to the top," said Comet. With that, they all headed for the volcano. On the way there, Asteroid commented, "It is very nice to have such good friends." They all agreed.

Once they reached the volcano, they looked up and could hardly believe their eyes. The volcano was *so tall* that they could not even see the top. Star, Comet, and Asteroid began to climb the volcano; and it started to become very cold. Thankfully, they were prepared and had their hats, gloves, and jackets. Lava rocks covered the outside and made it difficult to climb. They could see millions of stars shining bright in the beautiful sky. "It is amazing looking into the UNIVERSE from here," Asteroid said. Comet and Star agreed. They saw the two moons circling Mars, and off in the distance they could see other planets: Earth and Jupiter.

Comet wondered out loud, "Where should we go next?" "How about Venus?" said Asteroid. "Sounds good," they said. "It is so nice to travel through the UNIVERSE. I couldn't imagine anything better than this," said Asteroid. They had tons of fun and excitement on Mars that they could hardly wait for tomorrow. They all wondered where their next adventure would take them. Until next time!

CPSIA information can be obtained
at www.ICGtesting.com
Printed in the USA
LVIC040236011212
309598LV00003B